For Joe

First U.S. paperback edition 1997

The Library of Congress has cataloged the hardcover edition as follows:

Jeram, Anita.
Contrary Mary / Anita Jeram. — 1st U.S. ed.
ISBN 1-56402-644-2 (hardcover)
[1. Contrary Mary the mouse decides one day to do the opposite of
what she is supposed to do, but when her mother does the same, Mary
has a change of heart. 2. Mice—Fiction. 3. Behavior—Fiction.]
I. Title.
PZ.J467Co   1995
[E]—dc20   95-6304

1-56402-985-9 (paperback)

10 9 8 7 6 5 4 3 2

Printed in Hong Kong

This book was typeset in Columbus.
The pictures were done in watercolor and ink.

Candlewick Press
2067 Massachusetts Avenue
Cambridge, Massachusetts 02140

Contrary Mary

Anita Jeram

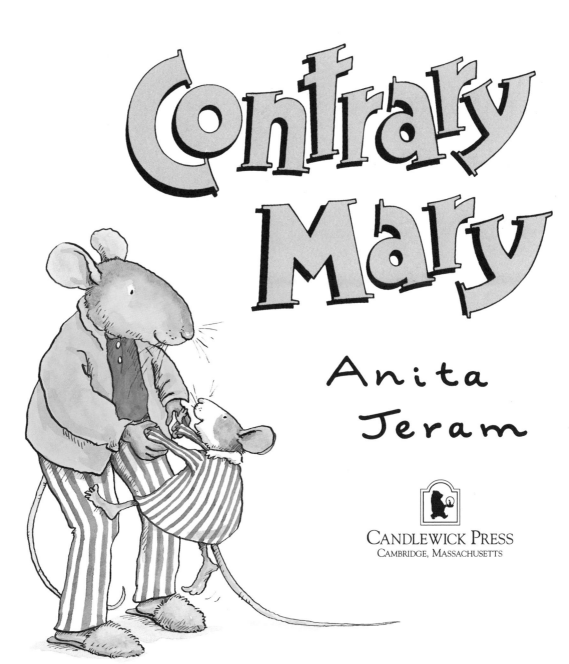

CANDLEWICK PRESS
CAMBRIDGE, MASSACHUSETTS

When Mary got up this morning, she was feeling contrary. She put her cap on backward and her shoes on the wrong feet.

"Are you awake, Mary?"
her mom called.
"No!" said Contrary Mary.

For breakfast there
was hot toast with
peanut butter.
"What would you like,
Mary?" asked Mom.
"Roast potatoes and gravy,
please," said Contrary Mary.

When they went
to the store,
it was raining.

"Come under the umbrella, Mary," said Mom. But Contrary Mary didn't. She just danced around, getting wet.

All day long,
Contrary Mary did
contrary things.
She rode her
bicycle backward.
She went for
a walk on
her hands.

She read a book upside
down. She flew her
kite along the ground.
Mary's mom shook her head.
"Mary, Mary, quite
contrary," she said.
And then she
had an idea.

That evening,
at bedtime, instead of
tucking Mary in right-side
up, Mary's mom tucked her
in upside down.

Then she opened
the curtains,
turned on the
light, kissed Mary's
toes, and said,
"Good morning!"

Mary laughed
and laughed.
"Contrary Mom!"
she said.

"Do you love me, Contrary Mary?" asked Mary's mom, giving her a cuddle.

"No!" said
Contrary Mary.
And she gave
her mom a
great big kiss.